Pete Seeger and Charles Seeger

The Foolish Frog

Illustrated by
Miloslav Jagr

Music adapted from an old song
Book adapted and designed from Firebird Film by Gene Deitch

Macmillan Publishing Co., Inc.
New York

Library of Congress Cataloging in Publication Data   Seeger, Peter, date   The foolish frog.   1. Folk-songs, American.   2. Children's songs.   [1. Folk songs, American] I. Seeger, Charles Louis, date joint composer. II. Deitch, Gene. III. Jagr, Miloslav, illus. IV. Title.   M1630.S   784.4'92'4   73-2121   ISBN 0-02-781480-7

It is assumed that the person reading this book will whistle or hum or sing the melody as it would be done by the various people and animals. —P.S.

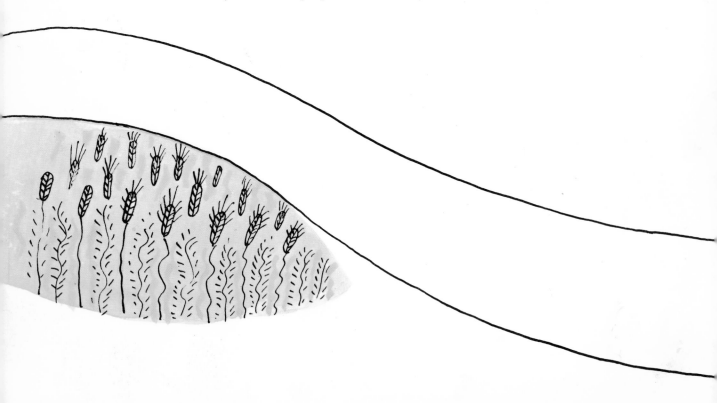

Once upon a time there was a farmer…
…walking down the road.
He was whistling a tune.

But he scratched his head and said,
"Doggone. I wish I had some **words**
for my song! All I've got
is the melody!"

Sound frogs make

River

Just then he came to a little brook.
And he leaned on the railing of
the bridge. Down there was a
big old bullfrog hopping
from bank to bank.

The bullfrog looked up,
saw the farmer, and thought he'd show off.

He took an extra special...

big hop!

Kersplash, he fell in the mud and got all dirty.

The farmer laughed
and laughed,

and started singing:

"'Way down south
in the yankety yank,
a bullfrog jumped
from bank to bank,
just because
he'd nothing better for to do.

"He stubbed his toe,
fell in the water.
You could hear him holler
for a mile and a quarter,
just because
he'd nothing better for to do!"

Now the farmer
went down the road
feeling very proud of himself
for making up a song.

...He went into the

CORNER ✶ STORE

bought some groceries, and said, "**Oh,** before I go home, I must teach you my new song!"

The storekeeper said, "Go home! I'm busy here. See all these summer people?"

"I won't pay you my money unless you let me sing my song!"

"Oh, all right. Sing it and get it over with!"

Well, the farmer started singing,
and the storekeeper shouted,

"Hey! That's a good tune!
Gather 'round, everybody, we'll have a party!"

And they were stamping on the floor,
drinking the **free** strawberry pop,
passing around the **free** soda crackers!

Back home, wives and children
were sitting down to eat supper
—and where's Father?
Mother says,
"Children, you'd better run down to
the corner store and fetch your old man.
He's probably wasting his time as usual!"

All the children
ran down the road
and ran inside the store.

When they heard the music,
they forgot all about
giving the message…

…and the children started singing:

"'Way down south
in the yankety yank...."

And the mothers were
drinking the **free**
strawberry pop,
eating the **free**
soda crackers, and

stamping on the floor!

Meanwhile, back in the barn,
all the cows said,
"Where is everybody?
We're supposed to be milked.
It's getting very uncomfortable!"

The cows walked out of the stalls,
they walked right out of the barn,
down the road, straight inside the corner store...

...and **they** started:

"Moo! Moo! Moo! Moo! Moo-moo-moo!
Moo-moo! Moo! Moo! Moo-moo-moo!"

The cows were stamping on the floor,
drinking the **free** strawberry pop,
eating the **free** soda crackers!

Out in the barnyard,
all the chickens said,
"Where is everybody?
We're supposed to be fed!
We're getting hungry!"

The chickens hopped over the
fence, hopped down the road,
hopped inside the corner store....

"Plk-pk, plk-pk, plk-pk-pk,
Plk-pk, plk-pk, plk-pk-pk!"

Feathers flying through the air!

The chickens were stamping on the floor,
drinking the **free** strawberry pop,
eating the **free**
soda crackers!

Meanwhile, all the barns started talking. They said,
"We feel so empty without any cows,
without any chickens!
I guess we'll have to go find them."

The barns picked themselves up off
their foundations, they galumphed
down the road, and they all
squeezed
inside the corner store, believe it or not.
Ever hear a rusty hinge on a barn door?
That's the way they sounded.
"Eee-ee, ee-ee, ee-ee-ee, Ee-eee-ee, ee-ee, er-rr-rr!"

When the grass was gone,
the fields were gone.
When the fields were gone,
the banks of the brook were gone.

The brook said,
"I don't have anything to **bubble**
between!"

So the brook
bubbled down the road,
bubbled up inside
the corner store....

"Bububdublbldububbledub,
a-bububdublbldububbledub!"

The brook was bubbling
up and down
the stairway!

The feathers flying

Everybody drinking the

The grass was growing out the chimney!

through the air!

The cows' tails swishing out the windows!

free strawberry pop, eating the **free** soda crackers, and stamping on the floor!

There was the bullfrog, in midair.

He looked down—
there was nothing underneath him.

He looked over—there was nothing to land on!

He said, "Where am I?"
The only thing left was the road.
He started hopping down the road.
"Hey, what's that racket
down at the corner store?

"Why, they're singing!
They're singing about **me**!"

And he was so proud,
he **puffed** himself up with pride.

And he **puffed**, and he

puffed, and he

puffed, and he

puffed, and...

POW!

He exploded in all directions!

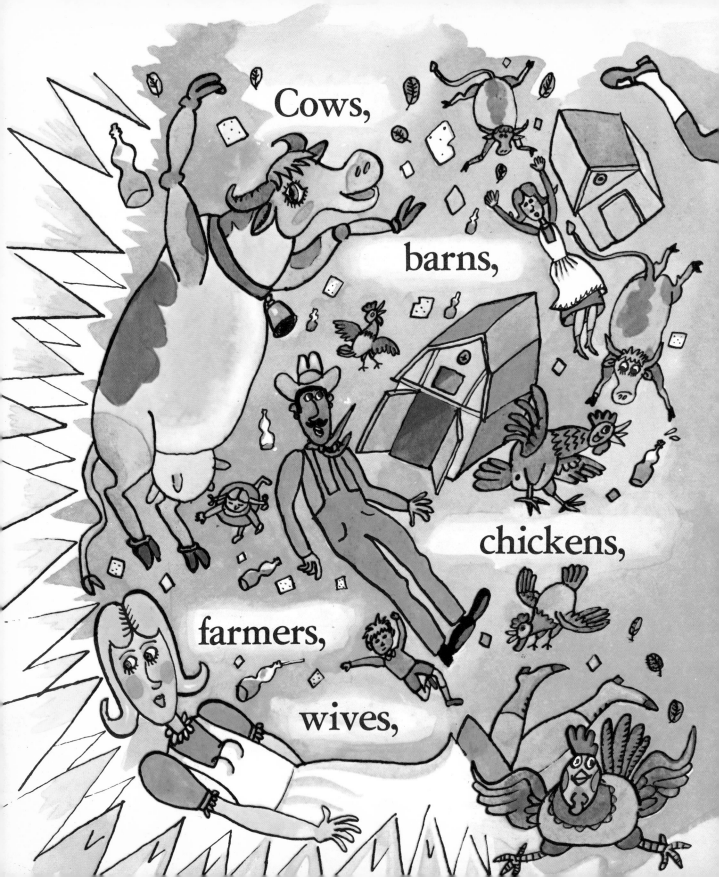

Cows, barns, chickens, farmers, wives,

They all landed right where they were
supposed to be the whole time—
sat down eating supper,
feeling kind of foolish for themselves.

Next day,
they went out to try
and find the frog.

They looked high,

they looked low . . . .

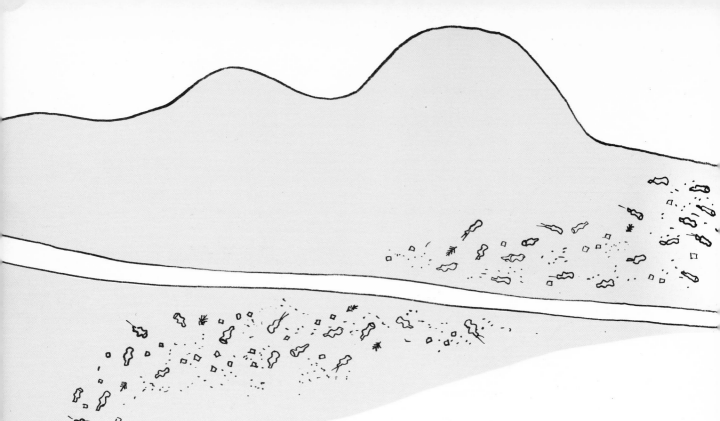

Strawberry pop bottles
and soda crackers in all directions—
but no frog....

So all there is left of the frog
is the **song**....

We might as well
sing 'er once again!

THE FOOLISH FROG

Can you whistle?

Turn the page

Whistle!

THE FOOLISH FROG

"'Way down south in the yankety yank,
   a bullfrog jumped from bank to bank,
   just because he'd nothing better for to do!

"He stubbed his toe, fell in the water.
   You could hear him holler for a mile and a quarter—
   Just because he'd nothing better for to do!

"There's lots of people just like
   that foolish frog of mine, frog of mine.
   Get themselves in trouble
   just to pass the time, pass the time.
   There's lots of people just like
   that foolish frog of mine, frog of mine—
   just because they've nothing better for to do!"

784.4   copy 1
SEE   SEEGER, PETE
    AUTHOR
    The foolish frog
    TITLE

DATE DUE	BORROWER'S NAME

784.4   SEEGER, PETE   copy 1
SEE
    The foolish frog